W9-CFB-826

READ ALL THESE

NATE THE GREAT

DETECTIVE STORIES

BY MARJORIE WEINMAN SHARMAT

WITH ILLUSTRATIONS BY MARC SIMONT
(*unless otherwise noted*)

Nate the Great
on The OWL EXPRESS

by Marjorie Weinman Sharmat
and Mitchell Sharmat

illustrated by Martha Weston
in the style of Marc Simont

Delacorte Press

SPECIAL GUEST APPEARANCES BY
Olivia Sharp, Willie the Chauffeur,
and Hoot the Owl
from the Olivia Sharp, Agent for Secrets series
by Marjorie and Mitchell Sharmat

Published by
Delacorte Press
an imprint of
Random House Children's Books
New York

Text copyright © 2003 by Marjorie Weinman Sharmat and Mitchell Sharmat
New illustrations of Nate the Great, Sludge, Fang, Annie, Rosamond, and the Hexes
by Martha Weston based upon the original drawings by Marc Simont. All other images
copyright © 2003 by Martha Weston.

Visit us on the Web! www.randomhouse.com/kids
Educators and librarians, for a variety of teaching tools, visit us at
www.randomhouse.com/teachers

Library of Congress Cataloging-in-Publication Data
Sharmat, Marjorie Weinman.
    Nate the Great on the Owl Express / by Marjorie Weinman Sharmat and Mitchell
Sharmat ; illustrated by Martha Weston.
        p. cm.
Summary: While traveling on the train to San Francisco with his cousin Olivia's owl,
Nate the Great and his dog Sludge must use all of their detective skills when the owl
suddenly disappears.
    ISBN 0-385-73078-0 (trade)   ISBN 0-385-90102-X (lib. bdg.)
    [1. Owls—Fiction. 2. Railroads—Trains—Fiction. 3. Mystery and detective stories.]
I. Sharmat, Mitchell. II. Weston, Martha, ill. III. Title.
    PZ7.S5299 Nawf 2003
    [E]—dc21
                                                            2002008264

The text of this book is set in 18-point Goudy Old Style.
Book design by Trish Parcell Watts
Printed in the United States of America
October 2003
10 9 8 7 6 5 4 3 2
BVG

To each other
and our long journey together.

—M.W.S.

—M.S.

To Marjorie and Mitchell—
with thanks for the great pleasure of getting to come
along on these wonderful trips with Nate.

—M.W.

CHAPTER ONE

Curvy Beak, Pointy Claws

I, Nate the Great, am a detective.
Right now I am a
clickety-clack
rocking-back-
and-forth
detective.
I am on a train.
My dog, Sludge, is with me.
He is a detective too.
We are on a case.
We are bodyguards.
For an owl.
Her name is Hoot.
She belongs to my cousin Olivia Sharp.

The case started this morning.
Sludge and I were visiting Olivia
in San Francisco.
Olivia is also a detective.
This morning she said,
"Hoot needs to take a train
to a special owl doctor
in Los Angeles."
"A plane is faster," I said.
"Hoot doesn't like to fly," she said.
"I, Nate the Great, say
that is a good enough reason
for an owl to see a doctor."
Olivia tossed her boa around her neck.
She always wears a boa.
"Glad you think so," she said.
Then she tossed her boa
around *my* neck,

looked me straight in the eye,
and said, "You'll take Hoot
on the train for me.
I know I can count on you."
Olivia pulled me over
to a covered birdcage.
She lifted the cover.

I looked into two huge staring eyes.
Then I saw a big head,
a curvy beak,
and sharp pointy claws.
"What big eyes she has!" I said.
"Yes, and she's easy to feed,"
Olivia said. "She eats mice."
"You have told me, Nate the Great,
more than I want to know."
But Olivia wasn't finished.

CHAPTER TWO

Wanted: A Bodyguard

"I will catch up with you later,"
Olivia said.

"How? Where? When?"

"When the time is right," she said.
"But for now, Willie will drive
the three of you in my limo
to the train station."

Willie is Olivia's chauffeur.
We had worked on another case
together. I knew him well.

"Anything else I should know?" I asked.

"Just one little thing," Olivia said.
"You'll be a bodyguard."

"What? Who am I guarding?"

"Hoot, of course."

"Hoot? Why does Hoot need a
bodyguard?"

Olivia handed me a piece of paper.

"Look at this," she said.

I, Nate the Great, read,

It will be
a happy day
when Hoot the
owl flies
away.
Your
neighbor

"Hmmm," I said. "Do you think
someone in this building
is trying to get rid of Hoot?"

"Yes, and I made sure
all the neighbors know that Hoot
will be on the train today.
So if the note writer takes the train
and tries to get at Hoot,
we'll catch him or her."
"Good plan," I said. "But why
aren't *you* Hoot's bodyguard?"
Olivia tossed her boa.
"Because my neighbors know
that I know
what they look like.
If they see me on the train,
I might scare them off.
That's why I need *you*!"
And that's how I, Nate the Great,
became a bodyguard
for an owl.

CHAPTER THREE

All Aboard

Sludge and I got into
the back of the limo.
Willie was already in the front seat
with the covered cage beside him.
I was glad it was not beside me.
Willie turned around.
"Miss Olivia wants Hoot
to get a good day's sleep," he said.
"So keep her cage covered."

"No problem," I said.

"But is an owl allowed on a train?
And a dog?"

"Miss Olivia took care of everything,"
Willie said.

"I believe it," I said.

Willie started the limo and we were off.

I took a pad of paper
and a pencil from my pocket.
I wrote a note to my mother.

Dear Mother,
I have a new case.
It is in a cage.
I hope to keep it
there. I will be back.
Love,
Nate The Great

When we got to the train station,
I handed the note to Willie.
"A note for your mother, Mr. Great?
I will send it to her."
"Thank you," I said.

On the train Willie carried the cage
down the aisle.
Sludge was sniffing.
People were staring at us.

At last Willie stopped at a door.
He opened it.
We went into a room.
Willie put the cage on a table,
patted Sludge, saluted, and left.
And there we were.
The three of us.
Hoot, Sludge, and me.

CHAPTER FOUR
Achoo!

The train pulled out of the station.
Sludge kept looking at the cage.
Was he trying to be a good bodyguard
or was he afraid of Hoot?
"I am going out to see
what I can learn," I said.
"Stay here and guard Hoot."
Sludge did not look happy.
I opened the door, walked out,
and closed the door behind me.
There was a room next to mine.
The door was open.
A man and a woman were inside.

"Hello," I said. "Do you know
an owl named Hoot?"
The man laughed. "Hoot who?"

I walked on.
Two boys were coming down the aisle.
"Do you know an owl
named Hoot?" I asked.
They laughed. "Hoot-toot-toot."

I walked on.
I saw another open door.
Inside, a lady was soaking her feet.
"Do you know an owl
named Hoot?" I asked.
"Yes. She lives in my building."
"I see," I said. "Is anyone else
from your building on this train?"

"Yes. Two men. One is a musician.
He's in the lounge. I don't know where
the other man is."

"Last question. Do you like Hoot?"

The lady scrunched up her face.

"She makes me sneeze.
Duck! I'm about to sneeze right now."

"Thank you for the information," I said.
"I will use it right now.
Especially the last part."

I ducked and rushed away.

I knew that lady had a reason
for not liking Hoot.

CHAPTER FIVE

The Look-alike

I walked on.
I passed rows of people.
They were sitting, talking,
reading, sleeping, or
just looking out the windows.
I found the lounge.
I saw a man with a guitar.
"My name is Nate the Great," I said.
"Tell me, do you like Hoot the owl?"

"Sure," he said. "She screeches.
And it's like music to my ears."
"Glad to hear that," I said.
"Now I'm looking for another man
who knows Hoot."
The musician smiled. "The Owl Man.
He looks like an owl.
He's sitting back there.
You'll know him when you see him."

"Thank you," I said.

"I'm writing a song about sounds,"
the musician said.

"*A wolf can howl without a towel
but sometimes needs to use a vowel.*"

"Well, have a good time
trying to rhyme," I said.

"Hey, nice rhyme," the musician said.

I walked back to where
people were sitting in rows.

I stared at everyone.

Then I saw a man
wearing a spotted shirt
and big yellow glasses.

His hair stuck up in two points.

The Owl Man.

I bent over him.

"Perhaps you like Hoot the owl?" I asked.

"Perhaps I don't," he said.
"People keep telling me
I look like her big brother."

I walked on.

Hmmm. Maybe Hoot did need a bodyguard.

Three people who knew her
were on this train.

Two of those people might not like her.

I went back to my room.

I opened the door.

Sludge was standing there.

With his ears perked up.

Like a good bodyguard.

He wagged his tail.

I looked at Hoot's cage.

It was just where Willie had put it.

"Fine job, Sludge," I said.

Sludge wagged his tail again.

"Time to rest," I said.

I sat down on a couch.

I looked out the window.

I saw trees going by.

And mountains.

And lakes.

I closed my eyes.

CHAPTER SIX

The Cage

I heard a voice.
It belonged to my friend Annie.
She was talking in rhyme.
"Do you know where you are?
Take a big guess.
You're asleep on this case,
on the Owl Express."
What was Annie doing on this train?

Then I heard a strange voice.
It belonged to Rosamond.
She is the only strange person I know.
She was also talking in rhyme.
"Don't snooze. Find clues.
Try hard. Bodyguard."
I sat up suddenly.
I, Nate the Great, had been asleep.
Had I been working on the case
in my dreams?
Why did bad rhymes get into my dreams?
Perhaps I was trying to give myself a clue.
I looked at the cage.
Was Hoot still asleep?
Was she hungry? Was she happy?

I, Nate the Great,
hoped the answers were
yes, no, and yes.
I got up and walked to her cage.
Willie had told me to keep it covered.
He had told me to let Hoot sleep.
But, I, Nate the Great,
had a job to do.
I lifted the cover.
Hoot wasn't asleep or hungry or happy.
She was gone!

CHAPTER SEVEN

Pancake Time

Had something happened
while I was asleep?
Sludge was standing by the door.
He would have barked or growled
if anyone had tried to come in.

I stared at the cage.
The cover looked
the same as before.
I peered inside.
There was a door,
and it was closed.

There were perches,
and they looked clean.
Everything looked clean.
Whoever had taken Hoot
had been careful to leave everything neat.
But who had taken her?
And how?
I needed time to think.
I needed pancakes.
"Wait here, Sludge," I said.

I rushed to the dining car.

I sat down.

A waiter came over.

"Has anyone ordered
a mouse to go?" I asked.

The waiter laughed. "A mouse?"

"Did you know there's
an owl on this train?" I asked.

The waiter shrugged.

"I heard people talking about it.
But nobody seems to have seen it."

I, Nate the Great,
was getting nowhere.

"May I have some pancakes
and one bone, please?"

"We have pancakes
with a wonderful fruit syrup,"
the waiter said.

"Fine," I said.

The food came fast.

I stared down at it.

The bone looked normal.

But my plate was dripping with syrup.

"Doesn't that look wonderful!"
the waiter said.

"No," I said. "It looks like a swamp
made of syrup."

The waiter smiled.

"This is a *blanket* of syrup.
The pancakes are tucked in under it."

"Tucked in? The pancakes are asleep?
Never mind. I'm hungry."

I ate and thought.
Did I have any clues?
Yes.
My biggest clue was that Sludge
is a great detective.
He had kept wagging his tail
as if nothing had happened.
As if no one had come into the room.
And I had other clues.
I finished my pancakes,

put the bone in my pocket,
and walked back to my room.
I opened the door.
Sludge wagged his tail.
I gave him the bone.
"We have solved the case," I said.
I picked up the owl cage.
"This cage is clean.
No stray feathers.
No bits or pieces of anything.
This is a new cage.
Never used.
Also, a waiter told me
that nobody seems to have seen the owl.
I, Nate the Great, say that
that nobody includes *us*!
You and I never saw Hoot
in this cage.
Because she was never in it!"

CHAPTER EIGHT

Sidetrack

Sludge looked puzzled.
"You're right," I said.
"We have not solved the case.
We still don't know
who wrote the note.
And we don't know why Olivia
wanted us to guard an empty cage.
She planned this well.
She didn't want me
to look in the cage.
That's why I was told that Hoot
needed a good day's sleep.

She told me about the mice
to make sure I wouldn't
try to feed Hoot.
And now, here we are,
you, me, and an empty cage
on a train
on the way to Los Angeles.
Olivia said she would catch
up with us. How could she
be sure of that?"
I, Nate the Great,
knew the answer.
Sludge and I stretched out
on a couch.

Good detectives know
when to take action
and when to wait.
This was a time to wait.
We waited. And waited.
At last a piece of paper
was slipped under our door.
I picked it up.
There was a message on it.

Olivia Sharp here.
In the private
car at the end of
the train.
Since you are a
great detective
you have figured
out:
(A) I have been on
this train all the
time.
(B) You are a body-
guard for a decoy.

"Come on, Sludge," I said.
Sludge and I walked to the last car.
I knocked on the door.
"Come in," Olivia called.
Sludge and I walked in.
Olivia was sitting behind a huge desk
with a computer, a telephone,
and piles of paper.

"I'm at work," she said.
"I'm writing up reports
on my last five cases."
"Where is Hoot?" I asked.
"Hidden on the train," Olivia said.
"Why didn't you tell me
the cage was empty?" I asked.
Olivia tossed her boa.
"Because I knew that
you and Sludge
would not want to guard
something that was nothing."
"Good thinking."
Olivia stood up. "So, did you
find out who wrote the note?"
"Yes. But Sludge and I must leave.
We will be back soon."

CHAPTER NINE

The Great Train Detective

Sludge and I were back
in ten minutes with
the lady with very clean feet,
the musician, and the Owl Man.
"Everybody please sit down," I said.
I turned to the lady.
"Hoot makes you sneeze.

But you sneezed when
I was with you
and Hoot wasn't.
So other things must
make you sneeze too."
"Yes," she said. "Turnips, glue,
petunias, dirty feet, cats,
chewing gum, anything pink,
fresh air, and spiders."
"Hmmm. So if Hoot wasn't around,
you would still sneeze."
"Yes."

"Then maybe you do like Hoot?"
"Nice owl. Good manners."
I turned to the musician.
"You like Hoot, correct?"
"Yes," said the musician.
I turned to the Owl Man.
"You do look like an owl," I said.
"But that's because you want to.
You wear spotted shirts,
you comb your hair into two points,
and you wear big yellow glasses.
You like looking like Hoot.

43

I, Nate the Great, say
that none of you
have a reason for
writing a terrible note about Hoot."
Then I turned to the musician.
"YOU wrote the note!"
"What?" The musician stood up.
"I did not write a terrible note.
I like owls."

"I believe you," I said.
Olivia walked up to me.
"Did you solve this case
or not?" she asked.
"Yes. I, Nate the Great, say that
the note was a get-well note!"
Olivia pulled the note
out of her pocket.
"It says that it will
be a happy day when Hoot
the owl flies *away*.
How can that be a get-well note?"
I turned to the musician again.
"You have a little trouble
writing rhymes, right?"
"Yes, and I needed something
to rhyme with *day*.
It was a good, friendly note."

"I, Nate the Great, say
that things that look good
to somebody
can look terrible
to somebody else.
Today I was served
food that looked good
to the waiter
and bad to me."
I turned to Olivia.
"End of case.
Hoot is safe."
Olivia tossed her boa
into the air.
"You were fabulous!"
she said.

"No," I said.

"Actually I was only great."

The boa landed on Sludge.

"I'll give you anything you want,"

Olivia said. "Make a list."

I reached into my pocket.

"Sludge and I came prepared," I said.

I handed Olivia a piece of paper.

"Now tell me *exactly* where Hoot is,"

I said.

"She's still on the train,"Olivia said.

Suddenly I, Nate the Great, knew Olivia

had given me a clue I did not want.

Sludge and I went back to our room
and sat by the window.
We were not alone.